4/03

# Palo Alto City Library

# My Red Rowboat

Written by Dana Meachen Rau
Illustrated by Miriam Sagasti

*Reading Advisers:*

*Gail Saunders-Smith, Ph.D., Reading Specialist*

*Dr. Linda D. Labbo, Department of Reading Education,
College of Education, The University of Georgia*

**LEVEL A**

**A COMPASS POINT
EARLY READER**

*For lake people*

## A Note to Parents

As you share this book with your child, you are showing your new reader what reading looks like and sounds like. You can read to your child any-where—in a special area in your home, at the library, on the bus, or in the car. Your child will associate reading with the pleasure of being with you.

This book will introduce your young reader to many of the basic con-cepts, skills, and vocabulary necessary for successful reading. Talk through the details in each picture before you read. Then read the book to your child. As you read, point to each word, stopping to talk about what the words mean and the pictures show. Your child will begin to link the sounds of the letters with the look of the words that you and he or she read.

After your child is familiar with the story, let him or her read the story alone. Be careful to let the young reader make mistakes and correct them on his or her own. Be sure to praise the young reader's abilities. And, above all, have fun.

Gail Saunders-Smith, Ph.D.
Reading Specialist

Consulting editor: Rebecca McEwen

Compass Point Books
3722 West 50th Street, #115
Minneapolis, MN 55410

Visit Compass Point Books on the Internet at *www.compasspointbooks.com* or e-mail your request to *custserv@compasspointbooks.com*

**Library of Congress Cataloging-in-Publication Data**
Rau, Dana Meachen.
   My red rowboat / written by Dana Meachen Rau ; illustrated by Miriam Sagasti.
     p. cm. — (Compass Point early reader)
   "Level A."
   Summary: A father and child row a red boat across a lake to buy groceries.
   ISBN 0-7565-0174-1 (hardcover)
   [1. Rowing—Fiction. 2. Boats and boating—Fiction. 3. Father and child—Fiction.]  I.
Sagasti, Miriam, ill. II. Series.
  PZ7.R193975 Myf 2002
  [E]—dc21                        2001004724

We take a trip
in my red rowboat.

We wear life vests

in my red rowboat.

We go to the market

in my red rowboat.

We row with oars

in my red rowboat.

We cross the lake

in my red rowboat.

We reach the dock

in my red rowboat.

The dock man watches

my red rowboat.

We put our food

in my red rowboat.

We head for home

in my red rowboat.

We sing some songs

in my red rowboat.

I love trips with Dad

in my red rowboat.

# Word List

(In this book: 37 words)

| | | |
|---|---|---|
| a | love | songs |
| cross | man | take |
| Dad | market | the |
| dock | my | to |
| food | oars | trip |
| for | our | trips |
| go | put | vests |
| head | reach | watches |
| home | red | we |
| I | row | wear |
| in | rowboat | with |
| lake | sing | |
| life | some | |

### About the Author
Every summer, Dana Rau takes a break from writing in her home office in Farmington, Connecticut, to go on a family vacation with her husband, Chris, and kids, Charlie and Allison. They visit a lake. Dana likes to take the rowboat out to the center and look at all of the beautiful scenery—the green trees, tall mountains, splashing fish, and soaring birds.

### About the Illustrator
Miriam Sagasti is a Peruvian-American artist who has illustrated children's books for more than eight years. Her whimsical characters and detailed illustrations are often executed in watercolors and colored pencils. Ms. Sagasti's work has been featured in textbooks, magazines, and even puzzles. She lives in Chapel Hill, North Carolina, with her husband and two dogs.